The Fugitive

J. M. DILLARD

Level 3

Retold by Michael Nation
Series Editors: Andy Hopkins and Jocelyn Potter

Pearson Education Limited
Edinburgh Gate, Harlow,
Essex CM20 2JE, England
and Associated Companies throughout the world.

ISBN: 978-1-4058-7691-9

First published in the United States of America by Dell Publishing 1993
First published in Great Britain by Signet 1993
This adaptation first published by Penguin Books Ltd 1996
Published by Addison Wesley Longman Ltd and Penguin Books Ltd 1998
New edition first published 1999
This edition first published 2008

3 5 7 9 10 8 6 4 2

Text copyright © Michael Nation 1996
Illustrations copyright © Bob Harvey (Pennant Illustration Agency) 1996
All rights reserved

The moral right of the adapter and of the illustrator has been asserted

Typeset by Graphicraft Ltd, Hong Kong
Set in 11/14pt Bembo
Printed in China
SWTC/02

Published by Pearson Education Ltd in association with
Penguin Books Ltd, both companies being subsidiaries of Pearson Plc

For a complete list of the titles available in the Penguin Readers series please write to your local
Pearson Longman office or to: Penguin Readers Marketing Department, Pearson Education,
Edinburgh Gate, Harlow, Essex CM20 2JE, England.

Contents

Introduction

Kimble stood up. He still had the guard's keys in one hand; he threw them away. He had a bad cut on one leg, but he knew one thing: he wanted to live now; he wanted to find the man with one arm, Helen's killer. He moved away into the night as quickly as he could.

One night a man with one arm goes into Dr Richard Kimble's house and kills his wife in the bedroom. When Kimble arrives home, he fights with the killer. But the man escapes. The police think Kimble killed his wife, and he is sent to prison. But Kimble escapes, and his search for the man with one arm begins. Kimble knows he must work alone. He needs a friend, but it could be dangerous to ask for help. And who exactly are his friends? Somebody is telling lies − but who? Somebody knows the true story − but will he ever find them?

While Kimble is searching for the man with one arm, other people are searching for Kimble. US Detective Gerard is looking for him, and he is only one step behind. Kimble has to work fast to find his wife's killer, because Gerard wants Kimble − dead or alive.

This is the story from the film *The Fugitive* (1993), a big Hollywood film with Harrison Ford and Tommy Lee Jones. The 1993 film came from the famous 1960s American TV programme, *The Fugitive*. In this programme Richard Kimble went all over the United States to find the man with one arm, and had a different adventure each week. The programme was popular in Britain, and other countries, for a long time.

J. M. Dillard has written many books from big Hollywood films.

Chapter 1   The Last Time

On the night Doctor Richard Kimble lost everything he went to a big dinner party at the Chicago Hilton hotel. His friends from the Chicago Memorial Hospital were there, and a lot of other people, drinking and talking.

Charlie Nichols, the most important doctor of the hospital, came across to him with another man. 'Richard,' he said, 'I want you to meet Dr Alex Lentz. Alex is working on the new drug, RDU–90. You know, he's doing all those tests for Devlin-MacGregor. Alex, this is Richard Kimble.'

'Hello,' Kimble said. But he was thinking, 'I've seen three damaged livers this week. They were all from dead people, and all of them took RDU–90. But in his report Lentz says the livers are all healthy. That's very strange.'

'Charlie says you want to talk to me some time, Dr Kimble,' Lentz said.

'What? Oh, yes,' Kimble said. 'Tomorrow morning, about your reports on those three livers. Will that be OK?'

'Right. Tomorrow morning.' Lentz smiled, but his eyes were hard and cold.

Kimble turned and saw his wife, Helen. He went over to her. 'You're looking very beautiful tonight,' he said. 'I love you. Look, you know I don't like these parties. Why don't we go home?'

'And I love you, too,' Helen said, laughing. 'But we must stay, dear. This dinner party is to get money for your hospital. Remember?'

The Kimbles stayed at the hotel for another two hours, then drove home. Just before they arrived at their house the car phone rang. Kimble answered, then he said to Helen, 'I have to go back to the hospital. Somebody's very ill.'

Helen kissed him. 'Go on then, dear. Be quick!' she said. It was the last time . . .

At the hospital Kimble saw another patient on RDU–90.

'I must operate quickly,' Kimble told the man's doctor. During the operation he saw that this man had a damaged liver, too. 'What's this RDU–90 doing to people?' Kimble thought.

The operation was quick and easy and the man was soon sleeping comfortably in a hospital bed. Kimble drove home, and phoned Helen from the car on his way. She was in the living-room with a book. After the phone call, she closed her book and went up to the bedroom.

At the top of the stairs she stopped. Somebody was there, in the bedroom. She walked slowly into the room and looked round. It was very quiet.

'I'm being stupid,' she thought and opened a cupboard to get her night clothes. A big hand came out of the dark and hit her hard in the face. She fell back on the bed. There was a man in the room, very big, dressed in black. She got to the phone; it was in her hand. The man shot her in the leg. She screamed. She tried to speak into the phone. Then the man fired again, straight at her head, and everything started to go black. She couldn't see, she couldn't speak . . .

Chapter 2   A One-Armed Man

When Kimble arrived home he looked for Helen in the living-room, then he went up to the bedroom. 'Helen?' he called. 'Helen?'

She didn't answer, but the light in the bedroom was on. Then Kimble saw the man and he ran in. He hit the man hard and his gun fell on the floor. The man tried to get the gun but Kimble held on to his arm. It felt cold and hard. He pulled the man's arm, and it came off! An artificial arm! The man looked at Kimble: dark eyes, dark hair. The man hit him hard and Kimble fell to the floor. The man took the artificial arm and ran out.

After a few minutes Kimble moved a little, and opened his eyes.

He pulled the man's arm, and it came off! An artificial arm!

Helen was talking into the phone. 'Richard . . . he's trying to kill me,' she was saying.

Kimble went to her. Her voice went very quiet. Her head fell back on the bed. There was blood everywhere.

'Oh, Helen, Helen,' Richard said, and touched her face.

'Richard . . . hold me . . . hold . . .' Her voice died away. The phone fell from her hand.

On the phone somebody said, 'Hello? His name is Richard, you said "Richard"? Hello? Hello?'

Helen was dead – Richard knew it. He sat next to her body on the bed and started to cry. Later, the police came. There were men and noise everywhere. They took him to the police station.

The police put Kimble in prison, and asked him lots of questions day after day. At his trial some months later they said, 'Kimble killed his wife. We can't find the man with the artificial arm. Kimble had the same gun that killed his wife, a .38 – and she said on the phone . . .'

'I didn't kill my wife!' Kimble shouted, but nobody listened to him.

After several weeks the trial ended. They sent Kimble back to prison. 'You killed your wife and you're going to die for it,' they said.

Chapter 3   Escape!

Kimble was in a bus on the way to Menard prison in Illinois, the place that they sent all the most dangerous criminals. There were two guards from the prison and another prisoner, called Copeland, in the bus.

'I'm going to die soon,' Kimble thought. 'But I didn't kill Helen!' He thought about the man with one arm.

'Hey! I'm hungry,' Copeland shouted. 'It's time to eat! You've got to give us food, and you know it!'

'Quiet, Copeland,' said one of the guards, a young man, but he got some food and came into the back of the bus.

Suddenly, Kimble saw a knife in Copeland's hand. 'Look out!' he shouted, but Copeland moved fast and the knife went into the young guard's side.

He fell to the floor and Copeland took his gun, but the bus was going fast and Copeland fired the gun accidentally. The bullet hit the bus driver and he fell dead. The bus went from side to side on the road, and Kimble and Copeland fell down on the floor. Copeland dropped the gun and it went across the floor of the bus into a corner.

'Hey! What's going on?' the other guard, an older man, shouted, and came into the back of the bus. Copeland went for the gun but the policeman shot him dead.

With a noise of breaking glass and metal the bus finally crashed on to its side and stopped. After a minute the older guard moved over to his friend. Then he turned to Kimble. 'You're a doctor,' he said to Kimble. 'Help him, he's hurt badly.'

Kimble looked at the man and said, 'we must take him to a hospital fast.' Kimble took the shirt off Copeland and pushed it hard on the big cut on the young man's side. 'This'll help,' he said.

Kimble heard a noise outside, and the bus started to shake. 'Where are we?' he asked. The noise grew louder and the bus was shaking harder.

The guard looked out of the window into the night. 'Oh, no!' he shouted. Kimble looked, too. They were on a railway line and the light of a train was coming very fast towards them. The bus started to shake harder and harder as the train came nearer.

Kimble ran to the back doors of the bus. He shouted, 'Give me your keys! Quick!' He thought: 'But do I want to live?' Then he saw the face of the man with one arm, and he thought, 'Yes! I do want to live. I want to find that man.'

The noise of the train came nearer and nearer. The guard threw his keys to Kimble.

'But which one?' Kimble shouted. 'This one? Tell me!'

The train was almost on top of them, as big as a black mountain.

'Yes! Yes! Quick!'

Now the light from the train was shining into the bus, and the noise seemed to be all round them. Kimble opened the door and the older guard suddenly pushed past him and jumped out.

'Help me!' Kimble shouted. 'Help me with your friend.'

The train was almost on top of them, as big as a black mountain. The bright lights on the front of it shone straight into his eyes. ('Do I want to live?') Kimble pushed the young guard out of the bus and jumped after him. They went over and over in the dark.

The train crashed into the bus. Metal and glass flew everywhere. Red and yellow fire shot up into the black sky through the tall trees. The train came off the line and stopped.

Kimble stood up. He still had the guard's keys in one hand; he threw them away. He had a bad cut on one leg, but he knew one thing: he wanted to live now; he wanted to find the man with one arm, Helen's killer. He moved away into the night as quickly as he could.

Chapter 4   The Search Begins

Detective Samuel Gerard looked at the train and the two halves of the bus. There were lights everywhere, a lot of police and a lot of reporters. Too many people – he didn't like it.

'Newman,' Gerard said.

'Yes, sir?' Newman was a tall young man, new to the police and he wanted to do all the exciting things, but Gerard gave him all the dirty jobs instead.

'Get down there,' Gerard said, 'where the train hit the bus, and look round carefully.'

'Yes, sir!'

'Poole,' Gerard said. 'You come with me.' Poole was a black woman, very strong, with hard eyes.

They walked across to some television lights – the old prison

'Kimble's alive!' Gerard shouted to all the policeman.
'Search every building and road in ten kilometres from here. Go!'

guard from the bus was there. He was sitting on the ground and speaking to the police and reporters.

'The prisoners are dead,' the guard said. 'I shot Copeland and Kimble died in that bus. Look at it!'

'Did you see Kimble die?' Gerard asked him.

'Uh . . . no, I didn't, but . . .'

'Then how do you know he's dead?' Gerard asked.

Suddenly, Newman ran up. 'Sir, I found these by the railway line.' He gave Gerard the keys to the bus. 'They were near the bus,' Newman said.

'Why were these keys by the line?' Gerard asked the older guard angrily.

'I . . . I gave them to Kimble . . .' the guard said.

'And he got out of the bus, didn't he?' Gerard told him. 'Kimble's alive!' Gerard shouted to all the policemen. 'Search every building and road in ten kilometres from here. Go!'

Gerard went back to his car and looked at the police photograph of Kimble: a rich man, intelligent, and there was something in his eyes . . . They were sad. Sad?

'Why did you kill your wife, Kimble?' Gerard asked the photo. 'You had everything. But I'll catch you. You'll never kill again, my friend.'

♦

Kimble arrived at the hospital in the early morning. He went in through a back door and found a room. A patient was in the bed. 'Hello?' Kimble asked, but the man didn't move or speak. Kimble went into the bathroom and cleaned the cut on his leg, then he washed and shaved. He put on some of the man's clothes – there was some money in the trousers – and the man's glasses. He found a white doctor's coat and he put that on, too, and walked out of the hospital.

At the door Kimble stopped to help some men to carry a patient into the hospital from an ambulance.

'We've just found him, doctor,' one of the men said. 'He was under that train. Is he OK?'

It was the young guard. The man opened his eyes and looked up at Kimble. He tried to speak: 'That's . . . that's . . .'

'This man's very ill,' Kimble said quickly. 'Take him to the accident department. Go now! Run!' The men carried the young guard away quickly. Kimble took the ambulance and drove away.

♦

Gerard was talking to Poole. 'Why do you think Kimble killed his wife?' he asked. 'Was he angry? Did he want her money?'

Before she could answer, Newman ran up and said, 'Sir, that young guard saw Kimble at the hospital!'

'What time?'

'9.30, sir,' Newman said. 'Twenty minutes ago.'

'Then he's still somewhere near here. Let's go!' Gerard shouted.

Kimble drove fast for a long time. He saw the Tennessee River hundreds of metres below. The grey and white water looked very cold. He drove into a wide tunnel. It went through a mountain by the river. There was light at the end of the tunnel, but suddenly Kimble saw a police helicopter and several police cars across the road behind it. Kimble stopped his ambulance in the tunnel.

'STAY IN THE AMBULANCE, KIMBLE. DO NOT MOVE,' a policeman shouted.

The tunnel was dark. Kimble got out of the ambulance quietly and tried to think. He looked back at the opening of the tunnel – more cars, more police. He looked round and then moved as quietly as an animal. There was water by his feet. He moved his hands over the sides of the tunnel and found an opening – it was a small side tunnel. He went in.

Gerard and Poole came down the big tunnel and looked into the empty ambulance.

'Where is he, sir?' Poole asked. 'Where's he gone?'

'He's near,' Gerard said. 'I can smell him. Poole, take a look down there, along the tunnel.'

There was light at the end of the tunnel, but suddenly
Kimble saw a police helicopter.

He jumped — down, down into the cold, dangerous water far below.

Gerard walked along slowly. He felt the sides of the tunnel, then he found the opening to the side tunnel and went in. He had a light in one hand and his gun in the other. He ran along the small tunnel, but the floor was wet and he fell. His gun disappeared into the water. Gerard tried to stand, but suddenly a strong hand took his, and Gerard looked up into that sad face, those sad eyes – Dr Richard Kimble.

'I did not kill my wife!' Kimble said. He had Gerard's gun.

'That's not my problem, Kimble. Now give me . . .'

'Sir! Sir!' Poole shouted in the dark. 'Are you there?'

For a second Gerard turned. Kimble turned and ran to the end of the small tunnel, but he suddenly stopped. Hundreds of metres below he saw the angry, white water of the Tennessee River.

'Kimble!' Gerard shouted. 'Throw down the gun and come here! You can't get away!'

'I want to live,' Kimble thought. 'But I want to find Helen's killer, too.' He turned back to the river below, ready to jump.

'Kimble! No!' Gerard shouted. 'You'll kill yourself . . . Stop! . . . Kimble!'

But he jumped – down, down into the cold, dangerous water far below.

Chapter 5   Help for Richard

'Now I know Kimble did it,' Gerard told Poole. 'I saw it in his eyes – then the man jumped!'

A policeman came up to Gerard. 'We've searched the river, sir,' he said. 'There's nothing. No body.'

'Look again,' Gerard said coldly.

'Oh, sir, there's nothing. The fish ate him.'

'So find the fish!' Gerard shouted.

◆

Kimble hit the river hard. He went under, down into the cold and dark, and the water pushed and pulled at him. He fought the water, and at last he came up to the top. He put his hand up to a tree and tried to get hold of it, but the river pulled him along too fast. After a long time the river went slower and Kimble was able to climb out. He lay on the side of the river and slept for a long time; then he walked to the nearest town. In a shop he stole some hair colouring. He went to the toilet of a garage, put the colouring on his hair, then he cut it very short. Outside there was a small bus with a family on holiday in it. The bus came from Chicago, he saw, and he quietly climbed onto the top. He wanted to go home.

Hours later the bus stopped at a café. Kimble was very cold so he climbed down and bought some hot food. The waitress in the café was nice and smiled at him, but Kimble thought the other people knew his face. He tried not to look at them. Then a report about him came on the television in the corner, with his police photograph.

'This is Richard Kimble, the killer,' a voice said. 'He died today in the Tennessee River after . . .'

Kimble left the café quickly and ran along the road. A car came up behind him and stopped. The police? The car door opened and a woman said, 'Where are you going?' It was the nice waitress from the café.

'Chicago?' Kimble asked.

'Get in.' She smiled.

They arrived in Chicago early the next morning and Kimble rang a friend, Walter Gutherie, from the train station.

'Richard!' Gutherie said. 'What are you doing? Where are you? This is really dangerous, you know.'

'I need money, Walter.'

'I can't do that,' Gutherie said. 'I have to think of my job, my family. Don't come to me or I'll get the police . . .'

Kimble put the phone down. In his office Gerard listened to the call – he recorded the calls of all Kimble's friends – and said, 'So he's

'Richard!' Gutherie said. 'What are you doing? Where are you?
This is really dangerous, you know.'

alive . . . and he's in Chicago.' He looked at Newman and Poole. 'Don't tell anybody. We'll get him.'

Kimble went to see Charlie Nichols next. He waited near Nichols's house for his car to arrive.

'Charlie!' Kimble said and Nichols stopped his car.

'Richard . . . I . . . So you didn't die . . .' he said.

'I need some money, Charlie,' Kimble said.

'Here.' Nichols gave him all the money he had. 'I'll give you more. Have this, too.' Nichols gave him his coat.

'Thanks, Charlie,' Kimble said. 'I must go . . .'

'Call me, Richard. I'll always help. You know that, don't you?' Nichols smiled.

♦

Gerard went to look round Kimble's house. He wanted to learn everything about the man. He looked at the phone in the bedroom and remembered Helen's words: 'Richard . . . he's trying to kill me.' Perhaps there *was* a man in the room, and perhaps Helen was trying to tell Richard about him?

He remembered Kimble's words in the tunnel, 'I did not kill my wife!'

Gerard shook his head. 'That's not my problem,' he said.

Chapter 6   Reports

After he spoke to Nichols, Kimble went to Cook County Hospital. He quickly found the department for patients with artificial limbs. Then he went to the cleaners' rooms. He found an open cupboard and took one of the cleaner's green coats with a name and hospital number on it. Then he left the hospital and went to a shop to buy some green trousers and some shoes. After that he found a cheap room to stay in. A woman and her son lived in the house. The woman took Kimble's money without any questions. The room was at the bottom of the house, it was cold and dark, and Kimble

Gerard went to look round Kimble's house. He wanted to learn everything about the man.

couldn't see the street. He felt very tired and he wanted to be ready for the next day, so he went to bed and slept.

◆

Gerard and Poole went to see Charlie Nichols in his office.

'I saw Richard two days ago,' Nichols said quickly.

'What did he want, Dr Nichols?' Gerard asked. He didn't like Nichols's face; it was too good-looking, too smooth.

'Help.' Nichols smiled. 'I gave him some money and my coat.'

'Dr Nichols,' Gerard said angrily, 'If you see Kimble again, tell him to come to me. That's the best help you can give him.'

'Never.'

'I always catch them, you know,' Gerard said. 'Always.'

When they were in the car Gerard said to Poole, 'Watch Nichols and tell me everything he does, everywhere he goes. OK?'

◆

The next evening Kimble went to work at the hospital as a cleaner. He washed the floors and slowly moved nearer and nearer to the department for artificial limbs.

'Where's Rudy?'

Kimble turned and saw a young woman doctor. 'Oh, Rudy's ill,' Kimble said. 'I'm doing his job tonight.'

The doctor went away. Kimble went into the offices. He wanted to read some reports and to learn about artificial limbs.

'Rudy!'

Kimble turned quickly and saw a woman. She had an artificial arm in her hand. 'Oh, sorry,' she said. 'I thought you were Rudy.'

'No, I'm cleaning tonight. I'll come back . . .'

'Oh, It's OK. I'm going to be here all night. I must finish this arm,' she said.

She went to her desk and Kimble went into a small room to get the reports. He took some of them and put them under his shirt.

'What are you doing in here?' It was the woman again.

'Uh . . . they told me to clean the windows . . .'

'Oh, OK. Do you want some coffee? I made a lot.' She smiled.

He took some of the reports and put them under his shirt.

'No, thanks,' Kimble said. 'I have to go.'

In the elevator he saw the young woman doctor again. He read her name on her white coat: Dr Eastman. She wanted to be friendly and said, 'How are you? Are you going home now?'

'Er, yeah,' he said. He didn't look at her, it was too dangerous, but he wanted to. He needed a friend.

Back in his cold room Kimble read all the reports and learned about artificial limbs. He wanted to know what to look for on the computer.

Chapter 7   Information

'I must get into the computer room,' Kimble thought, 'look at the reports, and finish tonight, or somebody will see my face and know I'm here.'

When he arrived at the hospital that evening Kimble saw a lot of police and doctors, and some new patients were coming in after an accident.

Dr Eastman was there; she spoke to him. 'This is bad – a bus came off the road. Take this boy up to a bed on the third floor now, will you, please?'

Kimble went to the elevator. The boy looked dangerously ill, so Kimble carefully touched his sides and his head. He decided that the boy needed an operation immediately. He wrote some information for the doctors on the boy's report, then took him straight to the operating theatres on the fourth floor of the hospital.

From the fourth floor Kimble went quickly to the computer room in the artificial limbs department. He needed to describe Helen's killer, so he put into the computer: MAN, 35–40 YEARS, WHITE, RIGHT ARM.

The computer answered: NUMBER OF PEOPLE: 75.

'75!' Kimble said. 'I must give it more information.' He put in: HOME: CHICAGO.

He needed to describe Helen's killer, so he put into the computer:
MAN, 35–40 YEARS, WHITE, RIGHT ARM.

The computer answered: NUMBER OF PEOPLE: 21.

'I don't have time to find 21 people,' Kimble thought. 'What can I do?'

Then he remembered — 'I broke the top of the man's arm. Perhaps he got a new one here.' He put into the computer: BROKEN ARMS:JANUARY 21 TO FEBRUARY 1.

The computer answered: NUMBER OF PEOPLE: 5. Kimble wrote the five names on a list and left the computer room.

Outside Dr Eastman stopped him and said, 'I went to see that boy, but he wasn't on the third floor. You took him straight to the operating theatres fourth floor, didn't you? Why? How did you know he needed an operation?' she asked him angrily.

'You told me,' Kimble said.

'No, I did not!' she said. 'Stay here. I'm going to get the police.' But Kimble pushed past her and ran for the door.

♦

Gerard sat at home and thought about Kimble: 'He came back to Chicago to find the man with one arm. Why? Hmm, two answers to that one. First, perhaps Kimble didn't kill his wife. He wants to find the man and bring him in to the police. OK. But second, perhaps Kimble paid this man to kill his wife, and it went wrong. Kimble went to prison but this man didn't, and now Kimble wants to find him and kill him . . .'

The phone rang. It was Poole: 'We've found where Kimble's living. We brought a young man into the station tonight – he sells drugs – he saw Kimble's photo and he says Kimble lives in his house.'

'Right, I'll be there . . .' Gerard said. He went to the young man's house and looked round the small room. He saw the reports from the artificial limbs department at Cook County Hospital. 'I'll get you soon, Kimble,' he thought.

When Kimble came home, he saw the police car in front of the house. He turned and walked quickly away into the darkness. He stayed in a cheap hotel that night, then in the morning he started to phone the five men on his list. The first three were not the man that he wanted. Soon he had only two names: Clive Driscoll and Frederick Sykes. Kimble rang Driscoll's number. His brother answered.

'Clive's in prison,' he said. 'He took some money from a supermarket – shot a man, too.'

'I'm a friend of his,' Kimble said. 'Where is Clive? I'll go and see him.'

'The prison near the train station,' the man said. 'He's waiting for his trial.'

Kimble put down the phone. He wanted to visit Clive Driscoll, but it was dangerous to go back to that prison. He was in there before his trial, too.

'Perhaps one of the guards will remember me,' he thought. 'But I've got to go.'

Chapter 8   Running Again

In the computer room at Cook County Hospital Gerard got the names of the 21 men in Chicago with artificial right arms.

'Talk to all of them,' he told Newman and Poole. 'I'm right,' he thought. 'Kimble is looking for the man with one arm. But does he want to kill him, or to bring him in to me? I must find Kimble first.'

♦

Kimble stood in front of the prison near the train station. It was a grey, ugly building.

'I don't want to go back in there,' he thought. 'But perhaps Driscoll is the right man.'

Inside he went to the elevator and the door opened – it was full of policemen. He got in and tried not to look at them. On the fifth floor he got out and went to the visitors' room. He thought about the night of Helen's killing, about the man's dark eyes, his cold, hard arm. Was it him here, now?

'Visitor for Driscoll? Table 7,' a policeman said.

Kimble sat at Table 7 and waited with his eyes down.

'Who're you?' a man said. Driscoll.

Kimble looked up and saw a small, black man – the wrong man! He stood up quickly and walked towards the stairs; he had to get out of the building.

At the same time Gerard, Newman and Poole walked into the prison to talk to Driscoll. Newman and Poole took the elevator, Gerard went up the stairs. A man ran past him down the stairs. Gerard didn't see his face, but he knew immediately...

'Kimble!' he shouted. 'Stop!'

But Kimble didn't stop. He started to run, then went through a door. Gerard found a policeman and told him to close all the doors out of the prison.

Kimble ran fast for the front doors. He remembered the night when the train hit the bus, and here was Gerard, the same as the train, very dangerous, very strong, coming at him. The front doors started to close. Behind him Gerard took out his gun and shouted, 'Stop!'

Kimble jumped through the front doors, but they closed on his foot. Gerard ran for Kimble, his gun ready, and the words went through his head: 'Not my problem... not my problem...'

Kimble pulled his foot hard – he couldn't move! He pulled again, his foot came free, and the doors closed. Gerard fired his gun seven times, but the strong glass in the front doors stopped the bullets.

Kimble stood up; Gerard walked up to the locked doors. Each of them stood at the doors and looked eye to eye through the glass. Then Kimble turned and disappeared into the crowds and the traffic.

He went across Chicago to Frederick Sykes's flat. There was a police car in front of the building.

'So Gerard *does* think there was a man with one arm,' Kimble thought. He went to the back of the building and climbed the stairs

*Kimble jumped through the front doors, but they closed on his foot.
Gerard ran for Kimble, his gun ready.*

to Sykes's flat. He looked in through the window. The flat was dark so he broke the glass and went in.

Inside the flat Kimble saw some photographs of Sykes's children. He picked up a photograph of a man, about 35, a policeman. He looked at the man's face – the face of Helen's killer. Kimble quickly searched the flat. He found an artificial arm, a right arm with a new top, and some more photographs. These photographs showed Sykes on holiday by the sea. In one photograph Sykes was standing next to another man. Kimble looked carefully; he thought he knew the other man's face, too.

After a second or two he said, 'It's Lentz, Alex Lentz! That doctor at Devlin-MacGregor.'

In a cupboard Kimble found some papers about Sykes's job – he was a guard at the Devlin-MacGregor building in Chicago. Now he understood everything. Lentz, and the other people at Devlin-MacGregor wanted Kimble to die because he knew that RDU–90 damaged people's livers. He was still alive only because he went back to the hospital that night – and Helen died instead of him.

'Helen, oh, Helen...' he said. For the thousandth time Kimble wanted to die, too, but then he thought, 'No, it's better to live and catch this man.' He picked up the phone and rang Gerard.

'Kimble here,' he said.

Everybody in Gerard's office jumped. Poole immediately started to search for the number that he was calling from.

'Are you coming in, Kimble?' Gerard asked. Poole already had the first two numbers.

'I didn't kill my wife,' Kimble said.

'Not my problem,' Gerard said. 'Where are you?' Four numbers now – Kimble was in the south of the city.

'Fifteen seconds,' Poole said quietly.

'I must find some more things first,' Kimble said.

'Are you coming in, Kimble?' Gerard asked. Poole already
had the first two numbers.

Gerard looked at Poole. He started to speak slowly, 'Now, listen to me, Kimble. I'm going to . . . Kimble! Kimble!' Gerard said, 'He put the phone down. Did you get the number?' he asked Poole. 'Where is he?'

'Sykes's flat,' she said. 'We have a car there now.'

Chapter 9   Finding the Right Answers

Gerard, Newman and Poole walked into Sykes's flat and looked round. Then Sykes came in.

'What's this?' he said. 'Who are you?' He was a very big man with dark hair. He was angry.

'Police, Mr Sykes,' Gerard said. 'A man, called Richard Kimble, was here today. He called me on your phone . . .'

'I don't know Richard Kimble,' Sykes said quickly.

'Oh, yes, you do,' Gerard thought.

'Oh, I remember,' Sykes said. 'He's that doctor, isn't he? The police questioned me when his wife died – because I've got one arm. Look, I wasn't in town that night!'

'Why did Kimble want to look at these, Mr Sykes?' Gerard asked. He showed him the holiday photographs.

'I don't know,' Sykes said. 'Ask him.'

They left the flat. 'Watch him,' Gerard told Poole.

◆

Kimble left Sykes's flat and took a bus. He thought about Sykes, Lentz, and Devlin-MacGregor. He remembered the reports from Lentz on those three patients' livers. 'Lentz was lying,' he thought. 'He knew those livers were damaged. Devlin-MacGregor can make lots of money from RDU–90, but I knew the drug was dangerous so they wanted to kill me. Lentz paid Sykes to do it,' he thought.

Kimble phoned Charlie Nichols. 'Charlie, I've found Helen's killer. Lentz paid a man to kill me because I knew RDU–90 was dangerous. Where is Lentz? I must find him.'

Nichols did not say anything for a minute. 'I'm sorry, Richard, Lentz is dead. He had a car accident last year.'

Kimble thought, 'How can I catch Sykes now?' Then he remembered. 'I sent a piece of those three livers to Kath Wahlund. She's a very good doctor, and I wanted her to look at the livers, too. Perhaps she still has the pieces. I'll go and see her.'

◆

In his office Gerard spoke to Poole. 'We're going to see Nichols. I think he helped Kimble to find his wife's killer – and now I know that was Sykes. Where's Newman?'

'Here, sir,' Newman said.

Gerard gave him the photo of Sykes on holiday with the other man. 'I want this other man's name. And find the phone reports for Kimble and Sykes for the past two years. Did they talk on the phone?'

◆

Sykes put a gun in his jacket. 'Lentz gave me some money to kill Kimble that night,' he thought, 'But Kimble got away, and I killed the woman. Too bad.' Sykes drank some whisky. 'Kimble went to prison and that was OK, but now he's out and he's trying to get me.' Sykes drank some more whisky. 'So now I have to finish the job.' He left the flat.

Chapter 10   Lies

Kimble went into the Chicago Memorial Hospital by a back door and spoke to an old friend, Mr Roosevelt. He worked in the reports department and had all the papers on RDU–90 ready for Kimble. Then Kimble went to see Kath Wahlund.

'Richard!' she said, smiling. 'It's you . . . !'

'Kath,' he said. 'Please help me.'

◆

In his office Newman looked at the photograph of Sykes and the other man. He wanted to do a good job for Gerard. He looked carefully at the man's shirt and read, 'C. M. H.' Newman thought: 'C for Chicago, and, er . . . , H for Hospital. Yeah, Chicago M. Hospital. M for Memorial! Kimble's hospital!' He left the office and went straight to the hospital.

♦

Gerard and Poole spoke to Nichols at the Chicago Hilton hotel. He was at a big meeting for Devlin-MacGregor. Gerard showed Nichols the photograph.

'Do you know these men, doctor?' Gerard asked. 'One of them is Frederick Sykes – he works at Devlin-MacGregor.'

Nichols looked carefully at the photograph of Sykes and Lentz. 'I'm sorry,' he said. 'I don't know either of them.'

♦

In Kath Wahlund's office Kimble looked at the pieces of the three livers.

'You see,' he said. 'All these livers are damaged because the patients took RDU–90, but here, in Lentz's report, he says that these patients all had healthy livers.'

Kath looked at the livers, too. 'Richard!' she said. 'All of these livers have Von Meyenberg's Complex.★ It's very unusual for three patients to have it at the same time. Lentz used the same liver for all his reports! Now you can tell the police that Lentz was lying about the livers, and wanted to kill you because you realized that RDU–90 was dangerous.'

Kimble read lots of other reports about livers and RDU–90. 'Kath,' he asked, 'when did Lentz die? Which month?'

'Oh,' she said, 'uh . . . August, last year. Why?'

'There are reports here from October, November and December,

★ Von Meyenberg's Complex is an illness of the liver. Only two people in 100 have it.

'Do you know these men, doctor?' Gerard asked. 'One of them
is Frederick Sykes – he works at Devlin-MacGregor.'

all with Lentz's name on,' Kimble said. He found the list of the names of the people who had money in Devlin-MacGregor. One of them was Dr Charles Nichols.

♦

Newman phoned Gerard from the hospital and told him the name of the man in the photograph – Alex Lentz. 'And, sir,' Newman said, 'Kimble was here an hour ago and took some reports about RDU–90. A man here, Roosevelt, gave me some more information – Kimble and Nichols both worked with Lentz.'

'Nichols!' Gerard said. So he *did* know Lentz. 'Good work,' Gerard told Newman. 'Now get me those phone reports.'

♦

Kimble got on a train. He tried to think, to understand, but he didn't really want to. 'Charlie Nichols was my friend, but he tried to kill me. No, no . . . ,' Kimble thought. 'I must find him. But what can I do then? Charlie doesn't know Sykes.'

He saw a man with a newspaper. It said KIMBLE IN CHICAGO on the front page, and his photograph was there, too. The man looked across at Kimble, then he stood up quickly and went to find a train guard. Kimble counted the seconds until the next station. How much longer?

Suddenly somebody was standing in front of him. He had a gun. Sykes. Kimble stood up, and at the same time, a train guard opened the door and came towards them.

'Hands up, Kimble,' he said. 'Sir, you can put that gun down.'

'No, sir,' Sykes said. He turned and fired four bullets into the guard. People started to scream. The driver heard the noise and stopped the train. Everybody fell to the floor. Sykes dropped his gun and it fell near the dead policeman. Sykes and Kimble both jumped for it, but Kimble got it first. He hit Sykes hard, then he held the gun in his face.

'Do it, Kimble,' Sykes said and laughed. 'Do it!' He laughed again. 'You can't! You're too weak!'

*He found the list of the names of the people who had money
in Devlin-MacGregor. One of them was Dr Charles Nichols.*

Kimble wanted to kill him then, to shoot Sykes in the head, to use the gun that killed Helen. 'No,' he thought, 'I won't kill him. I'll be as bad as Sykes.'

He hit Sykes hard with the gun, and Sykes fell to the floor. Then Kimble ran out of the train – the gun in his hand.

♦

Newman told Gerard about Kimble's phone calls. 'I looked at all his calls for the last two years,' he said. 'On the night of Mrs Kimble's killing, Kimble called Sykes from his car phone at 7.30.'

'That's it,' Gerard said. 'Poole! Bring Sykes in.'

'Sir,' Newman said. 'I thought Kimble didn't do it.'

Gerard looked at him. 'That's not our problem,' he said, but he understood Newman. Gerard was sorry to know about the phone call, too. He found Kimble's police report about Helen's killing, and read it again:

'. . . I took a taxi to the hotel, and arrived at 8.30. I gave Dr Nichols my car that afternoon because his car was in the garage. He gave me back my car keys at the hotel and I drove my wife home in my car at about 10.30 . . .'

'Nichols made that call,' Gerard thought.

Poole ran into the office. 'Sir! The police got Sykes in a train, There's a dead train guard, too. Kimble ran off with a gun.'

'No!' Gerard thought. 'Now every policeman in Chicago will be after Kimble, and they'll shoot to kill!'

Chapter 11   Out of the Dark

Kimble took the elevator to the top of the Chicago Hilton where Nichols was talking to the people from Devlin-MacGregor. He opened the doors to a big room and saw Nichols in front of a crowd of people.

'Thank you all . . .' Nichols said. His face went white, 'Richard . . . I . . .'

*Kimble wanted to kill him then, to shoot Sykes in the head,
to use the gun that killed Helen.*

'You what, Charlie?' Kimble shouted. 'You tried to kill me because I knew RDU–90 is dangerous, and you knew it, too? Is that what you want to tell these people?'

Suddenly, Nichols ran from the room. Kimble went after him. In front of a door Nichols turned and hit Kimble hard. He fell. 'I can kill you now, Richard. It's easy.'

On the floor, Kimble shouted, 'For money, Charlie. Helen's dead – all for money! You were my friend!' He jumped at Nichols and they fell through a fire door onto the fire stairs outside the hotel. They saw the lights of police cars hundreds of metres below them.

A police helicopter flew noisily above them, and its bright lights shone into Kimble's eyes. He couldn't see, he couldn't hear. Nichols ran down the stairs.

Gerard and Poole came up to the top floor of the hotel. They saw a lot of people round the open fire door.

'They went through there!' a man shouted. Gerard ran out into the noise and lights of the helicopter. He saw a man with a gun inside it. Below him Kimble and Nichols were fighting on the stairs. Suddenly, the man in the helicopter fired his gun. Gerard saw the two men fall off the stairs and onto the glass top of an elevator on the outside of the hotel. The helicopter lights moved over to Nichols and Kimble. Gerard saw them fighting on the elevator, two small black shapes far below. Then the top of the elevator broke, and Nichols and Kimble crashed into the dark through the falling glass.

Gerard ran down the stairs inside the hotel. He met Poole. 'Where did they go?' he shouted. 'Did you see?'

'Fifth floor,' Poole shouted back.

Gerard and Poole ran down to the fifth floor. They opened a door into a dark, wet room. Above them big bags of dirty washing moved slowly along strong metal lines to two washing-machines. Each machine was ten metres long and full of hot water. Gerard told Poole to go quietly along under one line; he walked between them.

'Kimble! Are you there?' he shouted. 'I know about Sykes . . . and about Nichols.'

The top of the elevator broke, and Nichols and Kimble crashed into the dark through the falling glass.

Suddenly a big bag came fast towards his head, and Gerard jumped away. 'Kimble!' Gerard shouted and he moved slowly along. 'I know Nichols had your car and he phoned Sykes on the night your wife died.'

Gerard stood between the hot washing-machines and thought, 'Perhaps Nichols is in here. Perhaps he's listening to me, too.' He shouted, 'Kimble, it's OK, come out, now.'

Kimble listened to Gerard. He wanted to stop running. He moved nearer to the sound of Gerard's voice.

Poole walked under a line of bags. She turned quickly when one of the bags came at her from behind. She jumped away, then held her gun in front of her and tried to see Kimble in the dark and wet. She heard Gerard shouting, and stopped to listen. Another bag hit her hard on the head and she fell to the floor. Charlie Nichols walked silently up behind her, took her gun, then moved back into a dark corner.

Kimble found Poole on the floor, and he knew that Nichols was near. He walked carefully along the side of the washing-machine and looked round. Kimble saw a man between the two machines. He was walking towards him. It was dark, and the man had a gun. Was it Gerard? Was it Charlie? Which man wanted to kill him?

He didn't move, didn't make a sound. The man came nearer, holding the gun out in front of him. He spoke, 'Kimble?' It was Gerard! Then Nichols came fast at Gerard out of the dark. He had Poole's gun in his hand.

Kimble thought quickly: 'Hey! Charlie!' he shouted. Nichols was surprised; he stopped. Kimble pushed one of the big bags at Nichols. It hit him in the face and he fell hard. His gun flew away into the darkness.

Gerard turned and saw Kimble. Gerard's gun came up. Kimble looked into his cold, hard eyes. He didn't move; he looked at the gun.

Gerard smiled. 'It's all finished, Kimble. It's OK now. I know Sykes killed your wife, and I know Nichols paid him. Come with me.'

Kimble pushed one of the big bags at Nichols. It hit him in the face and he fell hard.

Kimble looked down at Nichols. He felt his head carefully. 'Hmm, no blood. He's OK,' he told Gerard. 'And I found Poole – she's OK, too.'

'We'll go now, Dr Kimble,' Gerard said. 'You know, you have good hands. A doctor must have good hands.'

Kimble smiled. It was all finished. Now he could start to live again.

ACTIVITIES

Chapters 1–3

Before you read

1   Look at the Word List at the back of this book. Answer these
    questions.
    a Where do doctors *operate* on a *patient* – in a *theatre* or an
      elevator?
    b Which of these is a *limb* – your arm or your *liver*?
    c Which can be driven through a *tunnel* – a *helicopter* or an
      ambulance?

2   Read the Introduction to this book and answer these questions.
    Who:
    a is killed by who?
    b do the police think is the killer?
    c is looking for Dr Richard Kimble?

3   Look at the titles of Chapters 1–3 and the pictures on pages 3 and
    6. Answer these questions.
    a What is Chapter 1 about, do you think?
    b Who is holding the artificial limb?
    c Who is standing on the side of the bus, do you think? Why?

While you read

4   Write the answers to these questions.
    a Who introduces Dr Richard Kimble to
      Dr Alex Lentz?   ....
    b What company is Dr Lentz doing tests
      for?   ....
    c What drug have the people with
      damaged livers taken?   ....
    d Helen's killer hits Dr Kimble and runs
      out of the house with what?   ....
    e Where do the police take Dr Kimble?   ....

5 Put these sentences in the correct order. Write 1–8.

a The older guard gives Kimble the keys to the bus.   .....

b Copeland kills the bus driver with the guard's gun.   .....

c Copeland hurts the young guard with a knife but
doesn't kill him.   .....

d Kimble saves the young guard's life by pushing
him out of the bus.   .....

e Kimble, Copeland and two guards are going by
bus to Menard Prison in Illinois.   .....

f The older prison guard shoots and kills Copeland.   .....

g Kimble escapes because he wants to find Helen's
killer.   .....

h Kimble throws away the guard's keys.   .....

After you read

6 What do you think happens in the time between the Kimbles
leaving the party and Helen going up to the bedroom?

7 What do you know about

a Dr Alex Lentz?

b Helen's telephone call before she died?

c the guard's key to the back door of the bus?

8 Work with another student. Have this conversation.

Student A: You are Dr Richard Kimble and you are answering
questions about your wife's death at the police
station.

Student B: You work for the police and you are questioning
the husband of the dead woman. You think that
he murdered his wife. Try to find out his reason for
murdering her.

Chapters 4–5

Before you read

9 Look at the pictures in Chapter 4. What do you think happens to
Dr Kimble?

10 Read the title of Chapter 5. Who will help him? How?

11 Are these sentences right (✓) or wrong (✗)?

    a The old guard thinks that Kimble has died in the bus.   .....

    b After Newman finds the keys, Gerard orders the
        police to search every building and road in the area.   .....

    c After Kimble changes into a hospital patient's
        clothes and glasses, Gerard sees him.   .....

    d After driving away from the hospital in an ambulance,
        Kimble is stopped by the police in a tunnel.   .....

    e Kimble takes Gerard's gun inside a small side tunnel
        and jumps into the river far below.   .....

    f Kimble steals some hair colouring. Then he colours
        and cuts his hair in a toilet.   .....

    g The TV report says that Kimble died in the river.   .....

    h A waitress gives Kimble a ride to Chicago, and his
        friend Walter Gutherie helps him.   .....

After you read

12 How do Kimble's friends Walter Gutherie and Charlie Nichols act towards Dr Kimble when they hear from him? Why?

13 Why are these important in the story?

    a the guard's keys

    b the Tennessee River

    c the café waitress

Chapters 6–7

Before you read

14 Discuss these questions:

    a Why do you think Kimble has come back to Chicago?

    b How will he live and what will he do?

    c What will Gerard do?

15 Look at the pictures on pages 19 and 21. What is Dr Kimble looking for? How can he find his wife's killer?

While you read

16 Finish sentences a–e. Write 1–5.

    a After Gerard talks to Nichols, ...

    b Kimble works as a cleaner in the hospital because .....

    c Kimble does not take the boy to the third floor but .....

    d When Dr Eastman angrily questions Kimble, he .....

    e A drug seller tells the police .....

        1) runs out of the hospital.

        2) straight to the operating theatres on the fourth floor.

        3) he wants someone to follow him.

        4) he wants to get information from the department for artificial limbs.

        5) where Kimble is living.

17 Put these sentences in the correct order. Write 1–5.

    a After phoning the first three men on his list,
Kimble speaks to the brother of Clive Driscoll,
a prisoner. .....

    b Kimble spends the night in a cheap hotel because
the police know his new address. .....

    c Kimble wants to visit Driscoll in prison but it will
be dangerous. .....

    d Gerard goes to Kimble's room and he finds the
reports from the artificial limbs department of
the hospital. .....

    e Kimble decides to go to the prison where one
of the guards will surely remember him. .....

After you read

18 Who says these sentences? Why?

    a 'I always catch them, you know. Always.'

    b 'They told me to clean the windows.'

    c 'How did you know he needed an operation?'

    d 'He took some money from a supermarket – shot a man, too.'

    e 'I'm a friend of his. Where is Clive?'

Chapters 8–9

19 What do you think will happen when Dr Kimble visits Driscoll in prison?

20 Look at the pictures on pages 25 and 27. What is happening? Will Gerard catch Dr Kimble, do you think?

While you read

21 Circle the correct word in *italics* in these sentences.

    a Gerard tells Newman and Poole to talk to *five / twenty-one* men in Chicago with artificial right arms.

    b Gerard, Newman and Poole walk into the prison to talk to *Driscoll / Sykes* as Dr Kimble is walking out.

    c *Gerard / Newman* tries to shoot Kimble, but the strong prison doors close between the two men.

    d To Kimble, the *police car / ambulance* in front of Frederick Sykes's flat is a sign that Gerard is also looking for a man with one arm now.

    e Kimble finds a photograph and Sykes's artificial right arm with a new *top / hand*, which show that Sykes is Helen's killer.

22 What does Kimble learn about Frederick Sykes? Put a tick (✓) next to the correct answers. He:

    a is a policeman.   .....

    b knows Dr Alex Lentz.   .....

    c is a guard at the Devlin-MacGregor building.   .....

    d is Helen's murderer but he wanted to kill Dr Kimble.   .....

    e was paid by Lentz to kill Dr Kimble.   .....

23 Write the correct name. Who:

    a calls Gerard on Sykes's phone?   ....

    b lies about the damaged livers?   ....

    c can make a lot of money from RDU–90?   ....

    d phones Charlie Nichols?   ....

    e is dead?   ....

    f does Kimble send a piece of the damaged liver to?   ....

    g puts a gun in his jacket?   ....

24 Why does Gerard:

  a shoot at Kimble seven times? Does he hope to kill him, do you think?

  b always say and think, 'Not my problem'?

  c want to visit Nichols?

  d want phone reports for Kimble and Sykes?

25 Discuss with another student why Sykes wanted to kill Dr Kimble.

Chapters 10–11

Before you read

26 Look at the pictures on pages 33 and 35. What is happening?

27 Look at the picture on pages 37 and 39. Whose life is in danger? Why?

While you read

28 Which are lies and which are true? Write *L* for lie and *T* for true.

  a Nichols says to Gerard, 'I'm sorry, I don't know either of them.'   .....

  b 'Lentz used the same liver for all his reports!' said Kimble.   .....

  c Newman says, 'Kimble and Nichols both worked with Lentz.'   .....

  d 'You tried to kill me because I knew RDU–90 is dangerous,' said Kimble.   .....

29 Where do these things happen? Write the answer.

  a Nichols stops talking to the crowd and runs out of the room.
    ....

  b Kimble and Nichols are fighting first on the .... and then on the **c** ....

  d Gerard shouts to Kimble, 'I know about Sykes … and about Nichols.' ....

  e Nichols takes Poole's gun. ....

After you read

30 Why is Kimble's discovery of these things important in the story?
   a all three livers have Von Meyenberg's Complex
   b the date of Lentz's death
   c the list of people who had money in Devlin-MacGregor

31 For what reason do these happen? Why does/do:
   a Lentz pay Sykes to kill Dr Kimble?
   b a man on the train with a newspaper go to find the train guard?
   c people on the train start screaming?
   d Kimble decide not to shoot Sykes?
   e Kimble and Nichols find themselves in the room with washing machines?

32 Choose one or two adjectives to describe each of these people in the story.
   Kimble   Gerard   Nichols   Sykes

Writing

33 Imagine you are Dr Kimble on the afternoon before the party at the Chicago Hilton hotel. Write a report of your findings about the new drug RDU–90. In your report, give your opinion of Dr Lentz's report.

34 Write a newspaper report of Dr Kimble's trial on the final day when he is sent to prison for killing his wife.

35 Detective Gerard has been recording the calls of Kimble's friends. Write the telephone conversation between Walter Gutherie and his wife immediately after he speaks to Dr Kimble.

36 Imagine you are Dr Kimble and you are now a free man. Write a letter to your sister. Tell her about your escape from Gerard when you jumped into the river from the tunnel.

37 Choose either Kimble or Gerard, describe him and say why he is interesting.

38 Kimble sent pieces of the three damaged livers to Dr Wahlund. Write a short letter from Kimble to Wahlund to go with the package. Say why you are sending them to her.

39 Imagine you are Gerard at the end of the story. Write a letter to Dr Kimble. Ask him to forgive you for not believing his story. Wish him good luck for the future.

40 Write a newspaper report about Dr Kimble after he is free.

41 What do greedy people do for money in this story? Does this really happen in life? Write your opinion and give examples if you can.

42 Write your opinion of this book. Did you enjoy this story? Why (not)?

WORD LIST

ambulance (n) a special vehicle for taking ill people to hospital

artificial (adj) not natural

bullet (n) a small piece of metal that shoots out of a gun

county (n) an area of Britain, Ireland or the US with a local government

damage (v) to partly destroy

department (n) one of the parts of a hospital, company or government

drug (n) a medicine

elevator (n) a machine in a building that takes people up or down from one floor to another (American English)

fire (v) to shoot

fugitive (n) a person who is on the run from the police

helicopter (n) a flying machine that can go straight up and can stop in the air

limb (n) an arm or a leg

liver (n) the large body-part inside you that cleans your blood

operate (v) to cut open someone's body to repair something inside; this is called an **operation**

operating theatre (n) a room in a hospital where doctors do operations

patient (n) a person who is receiving help from a doctor or nurse

several (quant) more than a few

trial (n) the time when a court of law tries to find the answer to the question: 'Is this person a criminal or not?'

tunnel (n) a long hole under the ground or through a mountain

whisky (n) a very strong drink